W9-CUE-899

Henry and Mudge

AND

Annie's Perfect Pet

The Twentieth Book of Their Adventures

Story by Cynthia Rylant
Pictures by Suçie Stevenson

Ready-to-Read

Aladdin Paperbacks

New York London Toronto Sydney Singapore

For Leah Brown, our perfect pet-sitter—CR
For M.C., Ron, Owen, Huck, the fish, and the kitties—SS

THE HENRY AND MUDGE BOOKS

First Aladdin Paperbacks Edition February 2001

Text copyright © 2000 by Cynthia Rylant
Illustrations copyright © 2000 by Suçie Stevenson

Aladdin Paperbacks
An imprint of Simon & Schuster
Children's Publishing Division
1230 Avenue of the Americas
New York, NY 10020

Also available in a Simon & Schuster Books for Young Readers edition

The text for this book was set in 18-point Goudy.
The illustrations were rendered in pen-and-ink and watercolor.
Manufactured in the United States of America

20 19 18 17 16 15 14 13 12 11 10 09

The Library of Congress has cataloged the hardcover edition as:

Rylant, Cynthia.
Henry and Mudge and Annie's perfect pet : the twentieth book of their adventures / story by
Cynthia Rylant ; pictures by Suçie Stevenson.
      p.   cm.—(The Henry and Mudge books) (Ready-to-read)
Summary: Although Henry's cousin Annie likes his dog Mudge, when she gets her own pet she
decides that a bunny will be perfect for her.
ISBN-13: 978-0-689-81177-7 (hc.)
ISBN-10: 0-689-81177-2 (hc.)
[1. Rabbits—Fiction. 2. Dogs—Fiction. 3. Pets—Fiction.
4. Cousins—Fiction.] I. Stevenson, Suçie, ill. II. Title. III. Series. IV. Series: Rylant, Cynthia.
Henry and Mudge books.
PZ7.R982Heah 2000 [Fic]—dc21 98-20017
ISBN-13: 978-0-689-83443-1 (Aladdin pbk.)
ISBN-10: 0-689-83443-8 (Aladdin pbk.)

Contents

Annie's Wish

Henry and Henry's big dog Mudge
always visited Cousin Annie
next door.
Annie used to live far away.
Henry didn't see much of her.
But now she lived next door
and it was fun!

Henry and Annie rode bikes,
played Frisbee, and
traded comics.

And, of course, they petted Mudge
all the time.

Annie loved Mudge.
She loved his soft eyes
and his warm nose
and his big paws.
Annie wished she had a dog.

But her father was at work
every day.
No one would be home
to take care of a dog.
Henry felt sorry for Annie.
He remembered how much fun it was
to get a new pet.

Mudge had been the cutest puppy.

He was all round and rolly.

And very small.

Henry could pick him up

and kiss him.

Henry sure couldn't
do that now!

And Mudge was so short
that he could walk *under*
the collie down the street.

Not anymore!
Henry wanted Annie to
have her own pet.
He went to his parents
for help.

Soft and Dry

"Maybe she could
get a mouse," said Henry's father.
"Annie's afraid of mice,"
said Henry.

"What about a turtle?"
said Henry's mother.
"Too wet for Annie,"
said Henry.

"A crab?" said his father.

"Too hard," said Henry.

"A bird?" said his mother.

Henry shook his head.

"It might fly into

Annie's teacups," he said.

"Okay," said Henry's father,
"Annie needs a pet that
isn't scary, isn't wet,
isn't hard, doesn't fly,
and tap-dances."
"Tap-dances?" Henry giggled.
"I just threw that one in,"
said Henry's dad.

Henry's mother was thinking.
"I know!" she said. "A bunny!
It's soft and dry and
doesn't fly."
"And it doesn't have to be
walked like a dog," said Henry.

"Yes," said Henry's father,

"but can it dance?"

The Pet Store

Henry and Henry's parents
and Henry's big dog Mudge
took Annie to the pet store.
When they went inside,
birds were singing,
puppies were barking,
kittens were meowing,
and mice were squeaking.

But the bunnies
in the corner
were being quiet.
Quiet and careful.
Just like Annie.
"Perfect," said Henry's mother.

Annie picked up a
white baby bunny.
She had soft eyes,
just like Mudge.
She had a warm nose,
just like Mudge.

And she had something
Mudge didn't:
a little cottontail.
"She's so *cute!*" Annie said with a smile.

Mudge put his warm nose
up to the bunny's warm nose.
The bunny sniffed, sniffed, sniffed.
She seemed to like Mudge.

And when Mudge gave her
a big drooly kiss,
she didn't even mind.

Henry looked at his parents.
"We've found Annie's perfect pet,"
he said.
And they took the
bunny home.

Snowball

Henry's Uncle Ed made
a beautiful hutch for
Annie's bunny.

It was painted with
flowers and trees.
It had a little china bowl
for the bunny to eat from.
And soft bits of cotton
for the bunny to sleep on.
It fit Annie's room perfectly.

Annie named her bunny Snowball.
She played with her,
and sang to her,
and took her to Henry's house
for visits.

The bunny liked Henry's house.

She liked riding on Mudge's back.

Mudge carried the bunny

all around.

And when he got tired, they stopped for crackers.

Annie was so happy
to have a pet.
A pet just right for her.
"I love my bunny," Annie
told Henry.
"I know," Henry said. "She's soft
and dry and doesn't fly."

Suddenly the bunny went flying
through the air and landed
on Mudge's back.
Annie laughed.
"Maybe she *does*!" she said.